Alien Situations

Simon Robb

Published by Simon Robb

ISBN 978-1-7644613-0-6

1

Donna had a little circle of friends who lived together in a little house on the outskirts. A little run-down thing that nobody cared about. Donna, Jean, Madelaine and Carlos managed to get by. Some of them would have a job sometimes. Nothing special. Something menial. They foraged for food. They grew a little food that could survive the temperatures.

Sometimes Donna and her little gang said there was nothing left to do. There was nowhere left to go. It was just a case of trying to survive. That's what they said when despair was talking.

But despair wasn't the only thing that talked. Sometimes hope talked. Hope is a lousy word that's been abused over time. It's been really abused by those with power. There's nothing more depressing than a word emptied out like hope.

Donna had a list of shrivelled words. Even writing those words down made her sick.

Madelaine could scoop up poison words and spit them out with ease. She had an appetite for poison words and for the bland ones in between.

Madelaine was a performer. She performed for others, and she lived for others. Somewhere along the way, the real

Madelaine got lost. Living for others ruined her. It brought her so far down that she had to be reconstructed in a dark room. A room that was safe and free from stimulation.

There's only so much people can give before they collapse. It's exhausting existing for another.

One day the doctor told her they could do nothing else for her. 'There's the door. See you later.'

Madelaine wandered for a while. She wandered looking for a safe place to stay. She found a flophouse. She found a boarding house. She found a lousy job. She found Donna, Carlos, and Jean.

When Jean was young, he had nobody. He went from place to place. He was set free to scrounge and make it or die. Some wolves lived better than Jean.

Then one day he met a girl. Jean loved Helena, and she loved him. They were so in love. She called him Jean Le Reel.

Love dies and gets reborn, sometimes. Sometimes it just dies. Jean's love died. Jean's love died trying to save him. Jean's love died on a winding road on a mountainside. Jean's love sacrificed herself so that Jean could live past the car crash disaster. Jean carried the memory of the sacrifice with him, and he carried it with him to Donna, Madelaine, and Carlos.

Carlos used to say it was better for humans to just do nothing. To contemplate their footsteps. Their breath. The flow of the mental things. Contemplate the flow of mental things and do nothing. Just watch it go. Don't do anything.

Watch the human words flow on and on. That was his solution to the slow destruction of the earth. To the bad situation. To the disappearance of species under the rule of man. 'Just watch that,' he said.

Donna and her crew said they wanted weighty words.

They had uses for weighty words. They could make changes to the situation. Changes to the scheme of things. The big-time shit scheme that was killing the earth.

Donna and her gang had tried another word. They spoke the word 'violence'. It kind of sat there on the table when someone spoke it. They could see that it had power. It got a reaction. It had weight.

Violence was a word that sat there and didn't shirk away when looked at. You could look at that word all day long, and it would still look you straight back in the eye.

Donna and her friends wanted words like that. Strong words. Because the words arraigned against the earth were so powerful.

Donna had violence, but she said she wanted more words. Donna's crew wanted Earth words. They wanted the earth to speak and give them the words they needed.

2

Ham and Anita were educated middle-class humans. There were so many inhabiting the earth. Playing cultural games. Playing relationship games. Playing with things that really didn't matter.

Ham was a second-rate academic who wrote about ethics. He did some writing, and maybe some people thought it was alright. But that was about it.

Anita was a bit of a player in the local film industry. She'd produced a film here and there. She knew people. She'd done an interesting film once with a writer called Cain. Cain's film scripts had been pretty successful. He played it safe. He did the romantic comedy thing.

Ham was writing an ethical novel about the climate disaster. He was at a dead end. Anita suggested he get some advice from Cain. So Ham visited Cain to get some tips on being successful.

When Cain got home later that day, Anita asked him how it went. 'You weren't there for long,' she said.

'Some friend of Cain arrived out the blue. They had something they needed to talk about.'

'Who was the friend?'

'I didn't catch his name,' said Cain.

'What did he look like?'

'He was maybe in his 40s. Good looking but a little scary.'

'What was he doing there?' asked Anita a little more urgently.

'He dropped off a box or something and talked with Cain.'

'Think about his name. What was his name?'

'John or Jean. I can't remember.'

Anita sat up quickly and looked at Ham.

'That's Jean Jambon, I'm sure of it!'

'What kind of a name is Jean Jambon?' he asked. 'You're joking, right? Jean Jambon is a joke name.'

She was pacing around the room now.

'Don't mention him again,' she said.

'Who is he?' Ham asked.

'What did I just say? Don't mention him again!' She walked out to the kitchen, opened the cupboard door and took out the vodka. She poured herself a large one.

On the television was an old movie. John Wayne was searching for a girl. He was searching in lonesome places.

'That's what brings you down,' Ham said to himself. 'Searching in lonesome places.'

'Don't ever mention that person again!' yelled Anita, as she poured herself another.

John Wayne was a real man who wasn't afraid to search. That's what he said to himself as he heard the sound of glass being smashed against the kitchen wall.

3

Cain knew Jean Jambon from the old days. Jean seemed like the kind of guy who wouldn't live long. Cain and Jean were good friends for a time, then grew apart. He hadn't seen Jean for more than twenty years.

Cain had his house with Rebecca and a place in the country. He liked spending time there. He liked the isolation. In the country, he could go for walks. He could think about his latest romance.

Walking through the forest was good for him. Except for the time he found the body. That was a bad time. The body appeared to him late one night. He had gone for a walk on his own. Down by the water at the bottom of the bank. He saw something that didn't look right. He stepped down slowly. The bank was steep. The moon was out, so he could pick out the contours of the shape. It looked human. It was human. He moved a little closer to the body and saw the face. As he did, he gasped in horror.

He walked quickly back to his house. Rebecca was up. She looked worried when she saw him.

'What's wrong?' she asked.

'Something's happened,' he said.

He picked up the phone. Dialled the number. Told the police what he had seen. Where the body was.

He put his phone away and looked at Rebecca. 'There's a body lying down by the creek. It's Jean Jambon.'

When the police arrived, Cain led them to the place.

'The body was right there. I don't understand.'

The two cops illuminated the surrounding area with their torches.

'He was here. He was dead!'

'We'll do a search of the area. Then we'll take a statement from you,' said one of the cops. 'But at this stage, we don't see a body, and we don't see any evidence that there was a body here.'

The cops walked away. They searched the area.

Cain and Rebecca looked at each other. Rebecca could see the anxiety on his face. She didn't know what to think, but she knew Jean Jambon was trouble.

'The cops will find him,' said Cain.

Rebecca shook her head. 'He must have come here for a reason. What have you done?'

'Nothing!' Cain said.

'You call this nothing?'

When the cops finished their work, Rebecca and Cain quickly packed their things, locked the house and got in the car. They drove away into the night, thinking of nothing but the mysterious body of Jean Jambon.

4

Ham had a ticket for an amateur theatre show. Anita wasn't going. An old friend of his, called Jason, was still doing the theatre thing. He lived on his own. Worked as a cleaner in the daytime. Didn't have anyone special in his life.

On stage there was a couple. A man and his wife. The woman playing the wife seemed too young. A detective enters looking for answers about how to spell the name of a previous tenant. The old detective thing again.

Once the house lights came up, Ham applauded and then walked quickly to the bar for an after-show drink.

Jason was with the young woman from the show.

'This is Madelaine,' he said to Ham.

'A wonderful performance,' said Ham.

Madelaine smiled at Ham, then turned her head towards the door. 'My ride's here. Nice to meet you.'

Madelaine walked towards a man clad in leather, standing in the doorway. They embraced and kissed.

Ham looked uneasy. He had seen that man before. 'Who's the guy in the doorway?' he asked.

'That's Jean,' said Jason.

'Jean Jambon?' asked Ham.

'No, not Jean Jambon,' said Jason. 'Jean Le Reel.'

5

Madelaine and Jean sped through the city. Madelaine held on tight, and they left the city behind. The freeway led them deep into the mountains, past the farmhouse ruins and empty fields.

Jean and Madelaine arrived at the old house. Madelaine got off the bike. Jean wheeled it into the shed. A gravel path led to the front door.

'Are you ready for this?' said Jean.

Madelaine smiled and opened the door. Carlos and Donna were waiting for them. Donna stood up and hugged Madelaine and then Jean.

She turned and walked into the kitchen.

'Here we go,' she said as she walked back into the room with teacups on a tray.

Jean looked out the window. The moon was bright tonight. He could see the mountain tops and the deep darkness beneath the folds of the trees.

'We ready then?' asked Madelaine. 'Let's go!'

6

When Ham got home from the theatre, Anita was waiting for him.

'When you waste your time going to see that theatre shit, I really wonder if you have the first clue about what you are doing. I mean, do you? What was that piece of shit you saw? Who cares about that? Get a grip on reality! You're getting old. We're getting old. You don't have time to waste. Start dealing with reality. What have you got to say about the real world? Well? Say something!'

'You know I went because of Jason.'

'Jason is a loser! Are you mad? What other losers did you meet tonight?' She was yelling now.

'I met a young woman who seemed pretty smart,' he said.

'She's smart, is she? Is she attractive as well?'

'She is.'

'And she's in the play?'

'Yes. Her name is Madelaine.'

Anita moved a step closer to Ham. 'I don't care what her name is. You think you're interesting and attractive to young women? Do you think that? She's probably laughing about you right now. The old idiot who came to the theatre, who thought he had interesting opinions. I suppose you drove her home as well? Well, did you? Did she invite you in for a drink? Is that what happened?' She was up close now and in his face.

'I thought she went home with someone you know,' he said. There was a pause. 'I thought she went home with Jean Jambon.'

'You think that's funny, don't you! What did I tell you? I told you to never mention that bastard again!' She took a step back then slapped his face hard.

Ham walked to the kitchen and poured two drinks. He walked back to where Anita stood.

Anita took her glass and drank it down quickly.

She smoothed her hair, wiped her tears away and sat down on the couch. 'Jean Jambon is evil,' she said, 'and he used to be my life. Jean was a handsome guy. We met at university. I loved acting even though I wasn't any good. Jean was already part of the group. He was a year ahead of me. He was in charge of directing the show. He was acting as well. At first, he didn't really notice me. One night, there was a party at his house. After the show. The cast was there. Anyway, Jean and I got talking. We talked for a long time. Something happened. We started kissing. We fell in love. Just like that. It was crazy. It was so sudden. It came from nowhere. After that, we were inseparable. We spent a very beautiful time together. Then things started to fall apart for me. I was taking a lot of drugs. The only person I saw was Jean. I lost my friends. I lost touch with my family. And I got pregnant.' Anita stopped talking and looked at Ham.

'You never told me that,' he said.

Anita looked at him. 'I'm telling you now. Jean told me he never wanted a child, and it had to go. He said I had to get rid of it. He said he knew the child would cause his death. He was absolutely certain the child would cause his death. Like in some god-damned Greek tragedy or something. So he arranged for an abortion. But I couldn't go through with it. I had the child in a small hospital. In the mountains. On my own. It was horrible.'

Ham moved closer to her. 'What happened to the child?'

'Jean said that if I had the child, he would track it down and kill it. He said he would kill the child and then make me suffer.'

'What happened to the child, Anita?'

'I don't know! I don't know what happened to the child!' she said at the top of her voice.

There was silence in the room. 'Didn't somebody in the hospital tell you?'

'I told you I was on my own! Don't you know what that means? I was on my own! I was completely alone, and I was scared, and I was clueless!'

'I'm sorry. Didn't you want the baby? Surely you wanted the baby?'

'You're such a stupid man. What was I going to do? When I asked them, they said he was gone. The baby was gone! I should just forget about him! They had a car waiting for me. They made me pack my bag. A nurse walked me to the car. She told me not to worry. That my life would be a lot better now. That I needed to look after myself. Get some help.' She sighed. 'Just forget it,' she said. 'There is no baby boy. It's over. I've had enough. I'm going to bed.'

With that, Anita walked upstairs to the bedroom. She got undressed and fell into bed.

The cold made her shiver.

7

Madelaine, Jean, Donna and Carlos were deep in the forest.

'We need to be at the top of the mountain when the moon is at its zenith,' said Madelaine.

'You need to keep your eyes open. Your wild eyes and your wild ears open,' said Jean.

Donna led the group further into the darkness towards the mountain top.

Carlos was at the rear. 'Remember,' he said, 'if you see something that looks like a door, stay away from it. The door will take you away. You won't come back.'

The four stopped walking. Jean turned to Carlos. 'What do you mean, we won't come back?' he asked. 'What the hell is a door doing out here? What does that mean?'

Madelaine walked over and put her hand on his shoulder. 'We're going to be calm, and stay together, and we are going to enjoy this,' she said.

'Sure,' said Jean, 'but what about the door?'

'Just do what Carlos says. Do everything he says, OK?'

Jean held Madelaine's gaze.

'Don't worry,' she said. 'We're almost there.'

When they arrived at the clearing at the top of the mountain, Madelaine collapsed and started to cry.

'I didn't think I could do it. I thought I would never be here.' She wept freely in front of the others.

'It's alright,' said Donna. 'It's fine now.'

Carlos stood to one side. Gazing at the moon. It seemed so close. It glowed. Rivers of light poured down from it.

'It's so beautiful,' Donna said. The light flowed down on her. She stood there and let herself be bathed in it.

Carlos and Donna were entirely immersed in a river of love.

Madelaine clutched Jean's jacket. 'I want to go into the darkness. I want you to take me into the darkness!'

Jean looked at the others. They were gazing at the moon as it glided towards its zenith.

'We should stay here,' he said. 'With the others.'

She clutched his body tighter. 'Take me into the darkness now!'

Just then, she heard the beating of wings flying close overhead. An owl landed on a tree branch on the edge of the clearing.

'Now!' said Madelaine. She grasped his hand, and they slipped into the darkness.

Donna turned and looked nervously at Carlos 'Where are Jean and Madelaine?' she said.

Carlos scanned the clearing.

'They're not here,' he said.

'They were here a second ago.'

'Look,' he said, 'look right there!'

They were both looking now. Into the darkness in front of them.

'There it is!' said Carlos, in a terrified whisper.

A door moved slowly behind a tree trunk. As it moved, they heard Madelaine's cry for help coming from inside.

Two frozen faces were trapped in a deep shadow. Framed by a door. Their startled eyes shining in the moonlight.

'Do something!' urged Donna. Carlos stood up and rushed towards his friends. Their images vanished. The door ran down the mountain.

'Jean! Madelaine!' screamed Donna.

'They're gone,' said Carlos as he collapsed onto the dirt.

She saw Carlos on his hands and knees. She looked at the night sky. A lone plane flew slowly overhead. Something from the real world, so far away.

8

Ham undressed and got into bed. He lay there for a while. Anita turned around and spoke. 'I've been afraid of that bastard for a long time.'

'Of course,' said Ham. 'I won't let him get near you.'

'You already have, though, haven't you? You said you saw him at Cain's. Then you said you saw him at the theatre. How could you do that to me!'

'I saw someone at Cain's. I described him. What he looked like. You heard the description. It was you who said it was Jean Jambon.'

'And then you said you saw Jean at the theatre. Why would you do that? Why would you be so cruel?'

'I thought it was Jean Jambon. He looked like the man I saw at Cain's. But Jason told me his name was Jean Le Reel.'

She suddenly sat up. 'Are you trying to hurt me again? How old was this man?'

'He was in his early twenties.'

'So why did you say it was Jean Jambon?'

'They looked the same.'

She turned away quickly.

'You piece of shit! Do you know what you're telling me? I told you not to go to that theatre! Are you trying to kill me with this shit? Do you know what you're saying? You saw my son!'

9

Donna was breathing hard.

'We need to get out of here. It knows where we are!' She was yelling at Carlos now. 'I want to get out of here now. I need to get out of here. You can come with me or not. I'm going!'

Carlos quickly got to his feet. He followed Donna down the mountain path. She was running now. She was running hard through the trees and bushes in the moon-lit darkness.

Suddenly, a tall figure appeared on the trail. He stepped in front of Donna. She screamed.

Carlos caught up and stood panting behind Donna. 'Who the hell are you?' he yelled. 'What's going on here? Get out of our way!'

The figure stood on the track in silence.

Donna grabbed Carlos's hand and pushed past the figure. They ran. At the bottom of the track was a white van. The rear doors were open.

Carlos and Donna stopped. They tried to regain their breath. They bent over, breathing hard. The false dawn light was glowing around them.

Donna straightened up. So did Carlos. They looked around. Everything was deathly quiet. They looked in the direction of the van. Standing next to it was the one they saw on the trail.

Donna stared intensely at the van. Then her face relaxed, and her whole body went limp. She walked onwards as if in a trance.

'What are you doing, Donna!' Carlos yelled in desperation.

Donna now stood impassively by the figure who lifted his hand and placed it on her forehead.

From a distance, Carlos saw Donna collapse to the ground.

'What have you done to her!' yelled Carlos as he ran to Donna.

'I won't harm her,' he said. 'She's mine.'

Carlos knelt in the dirt next to Donna's unconscious body. He held her hand and sobbed. Then he got wacked from behind and blacked out.

10

Carlos lay on the floor of the van with his arms tied behind his back. Donna sat next to him.

'Wake up, Carlos. You need to wake up.' Carlos was really out of it. He kept sleeping even when the van hit a hole in the road and bounced around.

There was a small window in the back door of the van. Donna could see they were still in a mountainous zone. It was the afternoon. She'd lost some time.

She was tied up like Carlos, but somehow, she'd managed to sit up. She could see cardboard boxes and ropes. That's all. All she could hear was the sound of the van. Suddenly, it started slowing down. Then it stopped. Someone got out. They opened a gate. As the van moved off, Donna could see a long fence surrounding what looked like a farm.

The van crept up the hill. Then it stopped. The driver got out again. They walked away. Carlos was still asleep. Maybe he was sick. Maybe he had a concussion.

Just then, the van door slid open. Two people grabbed Donna's hands and feet. It was so fast. She couldn't stop them.

'Let me go, you bastard!' she yelled. 'You piece of shit! Let me go!'

They carried her inside the house to a small, empty room. She was dumped on a mattress and left there. They locked the door behind them. They walked out to the van and picked up Carlos. He groaned a little. They carried him into a different room from Donna. They locked the door behind them.

Donna put her ear to the wall. She was listening hard. She could hear Carlos breathing heavily. 'Carlos, are you alright?' she whispered. Silence. She tried again, this time tapping on the wall as well. She listened carefully. Just heavy, slow breathing.

She stood up and tried to look out the window. The sun was shining on a dry meadow. It looked like a meadow from long ago. Before the disasters.

She lay down on the mattress. She cried. She slept for a long time.

When Donna woke up, there was some bread in a bowl next to her mattress. And some water. She took the water and drank it down. She picked up the bread. She opened her mouth and slowly chewed it. 'They're probably not going to poison me,' she said to herself.

After she swallowed the bread, she put her ear to the wall. She listened for Carlos. It was very quiet in there. She couldn't hear any breathing.

She stood up. As she turned around, the door opened. Standing in the doorway was Jan. The figure from the van. Donna scanned his face. It was strange, yet so familiar.

'I want to see Carlos,' pleaded Donna. 'I want to see Carlos now!'

'Carlos is being taken care of,' replied Jan.

'He's being taken care of? 'What are you doing to him? What's wrong with you?'

'You both need fixing.'

On hearing those words, Donna's body became passive and obedient.

Jan led her down the hallway of the house. Into the super bright living room. In the living room, there were assistants. Donna had to shade her eyes. Donna could see the operating table.

'Lie down here,' Jan said.

Donna did what Jan said. She lay down on the operating table.

Jan held a long silver needle in his hand. He held it up to the light.

'What's the needle for?' she asked.

'I'm going to help you remember.' As Jan said that, he pushed the needle inside her nose. He slid it deep inside her skull.

Donna's brain lit up. She saw a thousand exploding suns. She saw bodies turn to dust. She saw the earth split in two.

All of this was like a movie. Like a movie all humans have seen. The movie about the end of the world. That movie was showing inside her head.

'I need you to see this,' said Jan. 'I need you to remember.'

Then Jan appears to little Donna at night. He appears in her room at night when she is a child. He is standing in her room, looking at her. He is emanating controlling rays. The rays try to heal the terror. The terror of little Donna. Jan can communicate without talking. Donna can hear him. Donna tells Jan that she wants him to go away. Jan says he will always be here. He says that he has always been here. Donna wants to call out to Mummy, but her voice doesn't work. Her voice has gone. Her voice will come back one day in the future. Jan says that he has Donna's voice in his pocket. He says he will give it back on a nice spring day in the countryside.

Jan levitates Donna's body. Jan levitates her body through the bedroom wall and out into the night and into a pure white room. Jan has always done this. Jan is always doing this to her. Jan wants her to play with the other children. The other children in the strange room. They want Donna to speak to them. Donna speaks with her mind. Donna doesn't want to get too close to them. The children are a little pale and listless. The children have lights that move and speak and giggle. The lights run around and hide. Donna gets up and chases a light. It runs and hides again. The children are a little more animated now. Donna looks out the window. She can see the entire Earth.

Then she's taken to a terrible landscape. Jan pointed to that landscape and spoke to Donna.

'This is what you will write about. You will write so you can understand. You will share your understanding with the others. When the others understand, they will act. When they act, they will help save the sweet Earth from this forsaken future.'

Donna turned her head away and closed her eyes.

'That's what you humans do. This is what it looks like after the catastrophe.' That's what Jan said.

Donna opened her eyes and looked. She breathed it in. The death stench.

'Down there,' said Jan, 'look down there.'

Donna saw the fallen buildings. She saw the dead. Donna was drawn downwards. Down the stony mountain. Down towards the ugly plain. She left Jan behind. She didn't care about her safety. She shook her head. She cried.

'It's all gone,' she said.

She looked up towards the mountain. Jan stood at the top of the mountain. He raised his hand and beckoned her. Jan transported Donna. She stood in front of him.

'Donna,' he said, 'the whole world is like this.'

'Take me back to my cell. I don't want to be here. I don't want to see this!'

'You can change this, Donna. Find the way with your words. With the right words. You know what that means.'

There was silence then.

'Why are you doing this to me!'

When Donna stopped crying, she opened her eyes. She saw Jan standing before her in the cell.

As Jan walked out the door, he said, 'Get the instruments ready.'

11

Ham and Anita were relaxing after dinner. The television was on for some reason. They had been talking about Ham's novel. His novel about saving the planet.

Anita got up and turned off the TV.

'You know, Ham, I was thinking about the language you use when you talk about your ideas. I was thinking that your language made me think about something stored in a museum. I don't mean something publicly exhibited. I mean something in the storerooms. Something that no one is interested in anymore. Something that languishes in the dark. That's musty. Something that no one wants to listen to or look at.'

There was silence after that. Then Ham replied.

'It's not archaic or pointless to want to consider how we can act against what is clearly wrong. It's called taking an ethical stand.'

'You have to do better than that. There's no power in that. The power has been drained away. Look around you. Can't you see what's happening? You're just being weak again. If you want to save the planet, you can forget about an appeal to ideas of right and wrong. Those with power and wealth are not interested in your ethical world. It makes no difference to them. They don't care about destroying the world. Why?

Because their wealth protects them. They can wreak as much destruction as they want because, and this is how they think, because their wealth insulates them from the chaos and misery they give birth to.'

Ham stood up and looked out the window, into the night.

'The only solution is violence,' said Anita.

Ham shook his head. Then he spoke.

'Do you want to live in a world governed by violence? Do you want to live in a world where the powerful are those who are the most violent? The most hateful? The ones who control others through fear, pain and suffering? That's just a hell scape. That's a failed state. A failed state fuelled by fear and suffering can't be the answer to any question. You have to use methods that align with your goals. If you want to live in a just society, then you have to use just means to achieve it.'

While Ham was speaking, Anita had walked to the kitchen. She was only half listening. She poured herself a drink. When Ham finished, she sat down again.

'You know you are going to be wiped away by the forces of evil. You will be rounded up and disposed of with the rest of the reasonable, kind and respectful people. Alternatively, you can just eke out your pathetic yet kind existence in some nowhere zone, suffering the heat waves, the plagues and the floods with the countless others. Who, by the way, have quite possibly just decided to move into your house anyway. In that case, you can join the displaced, respectful people who have been temporarily housed in the warehouses and camps. There's terror here. And fear. And shocking anxiety, and the powerful are still in power. Your desire for an ethical response to the situation we find ourselves in is just a form of appeasement. It's cowardice. The failed state is already here. The rule of terror is already upon us. It's more subtle than you can see. But it's here. Wake up. Start doing something and show us that you really understand. Jesus Christ, do you care about anyone except yourself? Your philosophy and your ethics are just another form of narcissism. Stop being a narcissist! Get over yourself! Buy a gun and kill these people!'

'You're not yourself,' said Ham. 'There's something wrong.'

With that, Anita stood up. She walked out towards the door. She slammed it as she went out. This conversation led nowhere. People had been talking like this for a long time. Nothing had changed.

She kept walking. Then she stopped.

'Jean,' she said out loud. She looked up at the sky.

She walked back to the house. Ham was tidying the kitchen. Anita walked up close to him. 'I don't care anymore,' she said, 'I don't care about anything. I need to change things. I need to change my life, or else I'm going to just wither and die. I have to find my son. I have to find Jean.'

Ham looked at her. 'Just tell me what you want me to do.'

'I need to talk to your friend Jason,' said Anita. 'I want to go to the theatre now.'

12

Carlos sat on the edge of the operating table. He looked around the room. His eyes darted from object to object.

'Where's Donna?' he asked. 'What's going on? Is this a hospital?'

Jan smiled. 'Yes, this is a hospital. You had an accident, and we're looking after you. Your friend Donna is here too. She's also recovering. She's hoping to see you.'

Jan moved closer to Carlos. He put his hand on Carlos's arm.

'Where is this hospital?' asked Carlos. 'What hospital is this?'

'This is called the familiar hospital,' said Jan. 'Lie down, Carlos, and we can get started.'

Jan gave Carlos a reassuring smile. Carlos did as he was asked.

'Just keep your head still for a moment,' said Jan. Then he slid the needle inside Carlos's head.

Carlos's brain exploded in light. Inside the light was a creature. It was Carlos's little cat. From long ago. When he was little Carlos. Little Carlos was at home playing with his ginger cat. Little Carlos was feeling hungry. Little Carlos put down the cat and then went into the kitchen. He opened the pantry door and found some biscuits. He opened the packet and took some out. He closed the pantry door and then moved to the kitchen window. He was just standing at the window and looking outside, eating his biscuit. Then he saw someone. He saw someone who looked like a man. A man who shouldn't be there. Little Carlos could hear the man talking inside his head.

The man said, 'Why don't you come outside?' Little Carlos could hear that voice.

He walked to the door. The key was in the latch. Little Carlos turned the key and locked the door. He looked outside, through the glass in the door. He couldn't see the man.

He walked back into the kitchen. The man was standing there. Smiling. That was Jan smiling.

'I'm going to show you something,' he said.

Jan pulled out the silver needle. Little Carlos had seen it before. Many times.

'I want to show you something important,' said Jan, and with that, he plunged the needle inside the brain of little Carlos.

'Hey buddy,' said Jan, 'I want you to meet some people. You will love them. You will love them very much. This is Donna, Madelaine and Jean. One day, all of you will do something very special together.'

Then Jan pulled the needle out. Little Carlos woke up on the kitchen floor. He looked around. He stood up. He looked out the window. No one was there. He went to the back door. He undid the lock. He walked outside. His cat was there. Sitting in the sun. Looking at him. He walked to the cat. Picked it up. The cat started to purr. As the cat purred, the light around little Carlos grew more intense until everything became overwhelmingly bright. Little Carlos became the white light.

Carlos opened his eyes. Jan was looking down at him. Carlos had returned. The procedure was complete.

13

When Ham and Anita got to the theatre, it was late. They walked into the foyer and then the stage area. A small crew were pulling down the old set.

'You looking for someone?' asked one of them.

'We're looking for Jason,' said Ham.

'He's gone home, mate.'

'Jason lives around the corner,' Ham said to Anita. Let's just walk there.'

When they arrived, Ham knocked on the door. Jason answered. He seemed confused.

'Ham. Anita. Come in.'

Down the hallway were newspapers stacked as high as a person. Ham and Anita had to squeeze past. He gestured for them to sit at the table. The kitchen was crammed with boxes. Every available space was taken up with boxes and newspapers. The only free space was around the table.

'We're trying to find Jean Le Reel,' said Ham. 'I thought you might know how we could get in contact.'

Jason looked at both of them. 'I don't know how to contact him. You should talk to Madelaine. She was the young woman you spoke with briefly after the show.'

Anita gave Ham a filthy look.

'Do you have her number?' asked Ham.

'Probably. I'll get my phone.' Jason stood up and walked down the hallway to his bedroom.

Anita was still looking at Ham. 'This place gives me the creeps,' she said in a whisper.

'He likes to collect things,' replied Ham. He looked around the room. Everything spoke of the past. Of the old days and musty times.

Jason walked back into the kitchen.

'Here's her number,' he said. 'She can be hard to reach sometimes. If that number doesn't work, let me know. I've got another way of getting in touch with her. Would you like some tea?'

Anita gave Ham a look that said no.

'We need to get going. I'll be in touch, Jason.'

'Next time I see you, I'll tell you about Madelaine. She's interesting.'

'What do you mean?' asked Anita.

'I mean, she's got interesting friends.'

Anita smiled nervously.

'Is Jean Jambon one of those friends?' she asked.

'I'm not supposed to talk about him,' said Jason, as he shifted his gaze away from Anita and towards the floor.

The room became cold. Ham and Anita were silent.

'Jean will hurt you if you go near him,' Jason said quietly.

'What happened?' asked Ham.

Jason turned and stared at Ham. 'Nothing,' he said.

He led them back through the dark house to the outside, where Ham and Anita could breathe at last.

14

Jan set up a writing desk for Donna in her cell. It was plain and simple and made of timber. It had a plain and simple chair to match. On the desk was a pile of blank paper, and a pencil for writing the right words. Donna started to write those words.

I'm in an apartment in a city. Carlos is on the couch reading. Carlos is reading and relaxing. Everything seems fine. I look out the window and down at the street below. It must be morning. People are eating breakfast. In the apartments opposite, children are getting ready for school. Everything is normal. I get a text. I check my phone. It's Madelaine. She's with Jean. We need to meet. In half an hour. At the coffee shop next to the park on the other side of town. Carlos and I get ready. We take the lift to the ground floor and hurry to the metro. It's not too far. The train is crowded. We get off at the park stop. At the coffee shop, Madelaine and Jean are waiting. They stand and embrace us. Smiling. So happy. It seems incredible. We can't believe it. The cars are noisy as they go by. Someone is exercising in the park.

Carlos takes out a package from his jacket and opens it. He hands around some photos. These are photos of men. We all look carefully at the photos. It will happen soon. We know that.

'This one plays golf on Sundays,' I say. 'He drives there by himself. The car park at the golf club isn't that full when he arrives. We could do it there.'

Madelaine places her photo on the table. 'This one always walks to the same restaurant on a Friday. He probably thinks it's good for his health. It would be possible to pull up alongside him.'

'I like this one,' says Jean. 'On Saturday, he takes his son to football.'

'Too many risks. It's too public,' says Carlos.

'They're all public,' replies Jean.

'It doesn't have to be,' I say. 'This one lives on his own. No wife or children. We just go to his house at night, get inside, and take him.'

'If we break in, he'll hear us,' says Madelaine. 'He'll retreat to somewhere in his house and call the cops. It's not a great idea. I say we pick this one.' As she spoke, she pushed the photo to the centre of the table. 'We take him off the street and throw him in the van. Unless you have a better idea, that's what we're doing.'

15

Rebecca thought there wasn't much life left for her. Since the diagnosis, it was ebbing away.

She got up from the bed. She walked to the room where she painted. She decided to start a new work.

She stood still. Composing herself. She looked at herself in the mirror. At her reflection.

'That's not me,' she said. 'That's my body. I'm somewhere else.'

Then she began to paint.

When Cain returned home that night, Rebecca was in her room, sitting on a chair and looking at her painting.

As Cain walked in, she told him that she had been thinking about the body of Jean Jambon. 'Oh, you know, like what the hell was that? I mean, we haven't really talked about it. Haven't you been wondering what that was all about?' She turned and looked at him.

'I don't see the point,' he replied. He sat down and looked at the painting.

'Maybe I had a hallucination. Perhaps he was just tired and had a lie down and then got back up and walked home. Maybe that's what he likes to do in his spare time. Go around pretending to be dead. Maybe he enjoys walking around the mountains, lying down in the cold, hoping someone finds his pretend corpse.'

Rebecca smiled. 'I've been thinking about it all day.'

Cain looked at the painting. He moved a little closer to it. There was the body of a woman. She lay on the ground of a forest at night.

'These colours are really... I don't know what to say.'

'They're ghastly,' she said. 'They're supposed to be.'

'Is that Jean Jambon?' asked Cain.

'When I was painting this, I started to think of the appearance of his body. I say the appearance because for me, he is an image. For you, he was something real. For me, he is an image that has a strange presence. Because of you. Because you gave a creepiness that an ordinary image of a person doesn't have. You animated that image. That's how I feel at the moment. Like an image. Like an animated image. That's why I've been thinking about Jean Jambon. About the body of Jean Jambon. I want to go back there. I want to go back to our house in the mountains. I need to understand what's happening to me. I want to understand what's happening to me before I die. I need to save myself before I die!'

Cain took another look at the painting and then turned to Rebecca. 'I'll pack the car. We'll leave tomorrow.'

16

Ham and Anita had to return to Jason's house. The number he had for Madelaine didn't work. There was a message about it not being a number. Check again. That sort of thing.

When Jason opened the door, he didn't seem surprised.

'Problem with the number, right? Come in.'

When they got to the kitchen, Jason told them that he'd been thinking about an address he had for Madelaine. He couldn't remember where it was. He had it written down somewhere.

'Why don't you help me look for it?' he said. 'It's in the cellar somewhere.' He smiled and asked Anita to move to one side.

'Sorry, the cellar entrance is right here.'

The door to the cellar was in the kitchen floor. He lifted the door. It revealed some stairs.

'Maybe use the torch on your phone. That's what I do.' Anita and Ham looked at each other and then got out their phones.

'This way,' said Jason, 'and please be careful.'

Anita and Ham followed and reached the cellar floor. It was cold. It was dusty. Some things had been here for a very long time. Dusty old men's coats and shirts. Trousers. Shoes.

'I'm not sure if it's in here,' said Jason. 'We might have to go in a little further.' As he said that, he shone his torch into what appeared to be an empty doorway leading down into darkness. 'Let's just go down here a little way,' he said.

Ham and Anita followed Jason as he walked slowly down the narrow passageway. The ceiling was getting lower the further they went on.

'How big is this cellar?' asked Ham.

'Quite large,' replied Jason. 'It was used in the war. They used to store things here.'

'What things?' asked Anita.

'I think it was used to store files or documents.'

'Is that all?' asked Ham.

'Maybe they were storing patients here.'

'Patients?' said Ham. 'What do you mean, patients?'

They stopped walking.

'There wasn't always a house here,' said Jason. 'My house wasn't always a house. It was a hospital in the war.'

'What about the patients?' said Anita.

'The patients were the ones who died. They were stored down here until they could be buried.'

'That's great,' said Anita.

She looked at Ham.

'We're almost there,' said Jason, 'I think it's in the next room.'

The room was smaller than the others. Its walls were lined with shelves. On the shelves were old cans of food. On one shelf was a file. Jason looked through it.

'OK, we can go now. I've got it.' Anita let out a sigh of relief.

Jason led the way out of the room. Down the long corridor and into the first cellar room.

Anita followed behind him. She walked through the door. Ham was some way behind.

Jason moved quickly to the doorway. He slammed the door shut, pulled out a key, and locked it.

Anita screamed and pulled at the door. 'What are you doing? What are you doing? Ham! Let him out!'

As Anita was screaming, Jason quickly walked up the cellar stairs, slammed the door, and bolted it shut.

Anita cried hard. 'Ham,' she yelled, 'what's happening?'

The door was so thick, she could only hear a muffled response.

'Ham, I can't hear you!' She heard the door being hammered by something. Ham was hitting the door.

'Harder!' she yelled. He kept going until he was exhausted. The door stayed where it was.

'Ham,' said Anita, 'I'm going to get us out of here. I'm going to do it.'

She moved around the room. Blindly. Feeling her way across rough surfaces.

'I'm going to kill him,' she said out loud. 'I'm going to stab his eyes out and cut his head off!'

Just then the cellar door opened. She could hear Jason's creepy voice.

'I've got a visitor for you,' he said. 'He's looking forward to seeing you again.'

Jason opened the cellar door wide. Anita looked up. She could see, silhouetted in the light, the hateful body of Jean Jambon.

17

Donna was pulled from her cell. Carlos was already in the hospital. When Donna entered Jan instructed the assistants to tie her down.

'Carlos,' said Jan, 'in the future you and Donna will have a child. The child's name will be Pearl. You will love your child as humans do.' Jan motioned to his assistant.

'Tie him down.'

Jan placed his clammy hand on Donna's forehead and then on the forehead of Carlos.

'You can see Pearl now, can't you? Pearl has two hearts. She has two hearts because she lives in two worlds. She lives in the world of the fallen planet, and she lives in the world of the birth of the new planet. In the world that has fallen, Pearl has been captured by a slave gang. She has been captured by a slave gang who use her in the way they use young people. Eventually, the slave gangs will sell Pearl to the eaters. You know who they are.'

Carlos and Donna saw Pearl in a room with other victims, waiting their turn. And after that, even worse, the terrible end of their daughter.

Jan showed Carlos and Donna what Pearl had to endure. He conjured images of terrible abuse. Time after time.

Carlos and Donna were both crying. They were crying big, weepy tears about Pearl and her suffering.

'You love Pearl, but you can't stop this suffering. This is just the way the world works now. The planet has fallen. I can cause you as much physical pain and suffering as I want,' said Jan, 'but I thought I would start the torture lesson through your emotions.'

Carlos and Donna were sobbing. Their bodies were wracked by big, sobbing jags. Jan gestured to an assistant who covered them both with blankets.

'The pain is just beginning. Recover your strength.'

Through his tears, Carlos spoke. 'What about the other world? You said there was another world!'

Jan told them the other world was waiting for them. The other world wanted them to come closer. Pearl was waiting for them in the other world. The other world wanted to love them.

'Donna will help you find it,' he said. 'Donna is taking you there. All you have to do is follow.'

18

Jean Jambon walked slowly down the cellar steps holding a candle. Jason followed close behind.

Jean placed the candle on a table.

'It looks like you've had a hard time, Anita,' he said. 'Jason will bring you some water.' He turned and looked at Jason. 'Won't you, Jason?' Jason nodded and walked back up the stairs.

'It's been so long, hasn't it?' Jean said. 'You know I've never stopped thinking about you. But look at you. You seem upset, Anita. What can I do for you?'

Anita looked at him contemptuously.

'Jean, I don't know what this is about, but you need to stop. It's insane. You're better than this. What do you think is going to happen?'

Jean Jambon moved closer to her.

'What do I think is going to happen? I think that we are going to talk, and then after a while, you're going to tell me something that I want to know. After that, who knows? It's been such a long time. There's so much to catch up on. You know, I heard something strange, and I couldn't believe it at first. It really made me wonder what was going on. It made me doubt you, Anita. It made me upset and a little angry. Do you know what that might have been, Anita?'

She looked at Jean and remained silent.

'I'm waiting, Anita. I'm waiting for your answer.'

At that moment, Jason's footsteps could be heard. He reached the bottom of the stairs and placed the glass of water next to Anita.

'Jason here told me about someone called Jean Le Reel. It seems that Jean Le Reel is the boyfriend of an actor Jason knows. A very good actor, apparently. This actor's boyfriend is apparently quite good-looking. In fact, Jason told me that he looks remarkably like me. I asked Jason how old this boy was. Isn't that right, Jason?

Jason nodded.

'Do you know what he said? He said this boy's age was twenty. And how did he know that? How did you know that, Jason?'

'She said they were the same age. Madelaine is twenty.'

Jean turned and looked at Anita.

'The same age. Isn't that lovely? What a lovely couple. What a wonderful age to be in love. And then I started thinking about the number twenty. I started thinking about you. I thought about you and me, Anita. How in love we were. Until we had the problem. You know the problem, don't you?' Jean picked up the glass of water and drank a little. He offered some to Anita. She shook her head. He put the glass down.

'The pregnancy problem, Anita. I remember we had an agreement. I remember we agreed that you would terminate that problem. We had a very solemn agreement for the termination of that pregnancy. I made it very clear to you, Anita, that under no circumstances could that problem be allowed to be born. I made it extremely clear that you were to have an abortion.'

He paused and smiled. He turned to Jason.

'Do you know what she did then? She just disappeared. Can you imagine that? Disappearing when she has an important job to do. Very disappointing.'

Jason shook his head.

Jean suddenly stood up. 'And when was this? That's right! Twenty years ago! You had the child who should be dead!'

Jean sat down again. There was a silence. He smoothed his hair. Took a deep breath and then released it.

'Anita, I know you had the child. Tell me, who helped you back then?'

Anita looked at Jean Jambon in disgust.

'What's their name?'

Jean tried to keep calm. But this time he couldn't. He learned forward and wrapped his hands around Anita's throat and started to squeeze.

'Tell me his name,' he said through gritted teeth. 'Tell me his name, and I'll let you go.'

Anita struggled against him. They fell, smashing the glass of water and knocking the candle to the ground. They were in total darkness now. Anita couldn't take it any longer.

'Cain!' she yelled. 'His name was Cain!' With that, Jean Jambon loosened his grip. Jason fumbled for some matches and the candle. He lit the candle and held it near the prone body of Anita.

She looked around the room. Jean Jambon was gone.

19

We drove through the city traffic with the abductee in the back of the van. He was bound and gagged. We didn't want to hear his ugly talk. We'd heard enough already.

I drove the van to the house at the foot of the mountains. Madelaine opened the door. Jean and Carlos dragged him from the van and into the house. A little room had been prepared. The windows were painted black. It was almost empty. There were some chairs and some chains. The chains were fixed to the wall.

We dragged him into the room and dropped him on the floor. Carlos and Jean walked out of the room and closed the door. They joined Madelaine and me in the lounge room.

I spoke first. 'We can rest and then start working on him after that."

Jean stood up. 'No, I don't agree,' he said. 'We should start now. That way, we can maximise the shock to the public.'

I shook my head. 'Our target isn't the public, it's the cabalists. The public doesn't need any more terror.'

Jean walked to the kitchen. 'You say they don't need any more terror, but that's not true, is it? They actually haven't had this kind of terror. They've been the victims. We're changing that. What we're doing is the opposite of that. We're the agents of terror. On their behalf. The agency of the people is embodied in us. We are the agents of the will of the people, and that will demands terror!'

'So, what are you saying, Jean?' I asked.

'I'm saying that we go in there now and start working on him. We record it. Then we distribute it.'

Madelaine was getting frustrated. She looked at me.

'What are we even having this conversation for?' she said. She stood up and walked to the little room. Jean followed.

'Jean, get out your phone,' she said.

She walked over to the man lying on the floor.

'Listen, you piece of shit, we are going to hurt you, and we are going to record it, and then we are going to show it to millions of people. You thought you could abuse the earth and live a beautiful life. Well, that's over now. We are going to show you what happens when you abuse this planet. You and those others are finished. The cabalists are all going to learn about suffering, big time! You're the first. Your kind are going to be hurt until you decide to change. You're going to change, or we are just going to come and take everything. Your beautiful homes. Your lovely families. Your profits. If you don't change, we going to smash it all.'

She turned to Jean. 'Start filming.'

Jean started filming.

'Carlos, get over here and hold his hand against the floor,' Madelaine insisted.

The man's eyes widened. There were muffled sounds of panic.

'Get in closer, Jean,' she said. As he got closer, he could see that Madelaine held a knife.

'How do you like this, you piece of shit!'

As she said that, she sliced a finger from his hand.

'Now film his face!'

20

Some people went to the mountains for relaxation, but that's not why Cain and Rebecca were there. It was hard to relax in the mountains anyway. There was the constant threat of fires. Cain and Rebecca's little house was vulnerable. It was surrounded by an impenetrable forest of dark trees. The floor of the forest was in a constant gloom, broken by the occasional ray of sunshine.

Rebecca was immersed in a similar darkness. The darkness of her approaching death. The darkness of the collapse of her life on this earth.

Cain tended to her. He tended to her in a loving way.

'I want to see his body,' she said to Cain. 'I want you to make the body of Jean Jambon appear. I want you to make him present again. I want you to search inside yourself and find his body!'

Cain lit the candles. He drew back the lounge room curtains and saw the storm surging outside.

'You need to do this for me. You need to make this happen. I want to know that the dead can come back. I need to know I can come back to you. Cain, hold me and do this for me!'

Cain held her tight. Lightning split the sky. The heavens exploded in light and fury.

They turned and looked out the window.

Standing in the night was the sodden and bloodied form of Jean Jambon.

21

Anita was in a pretty bad way. Jean Jambon had held his filthy hands around her neck. She had to get her head straight. Jean Jambon could be anywhere. Ham wasn't making a sound.

The candle spluttered away in the gloom. Jason stood above her. She needed to make her move.

'I'm going to sit down on this chair, alright?' She stood up, picked up the chair and then sat down. 'I need some water.'

Jason looked at her warily.

'I'm exhausted. Please get me some water.'

Jason shook his head.

'What's the problem? What am I going to do? And by the way, where is Jean?'

Jason looked confused. 'He's somewhere else.'

'You don't know where he is, do you?' There was a silence. 'How long have you known him?'

Silence again.

'Because I've known him for a long time. In fact, I have known him for a very long time. He's obviously changed since I knew him. He was very charming then. Did something bad happen to Jean? Did something very bad happen to him?'

'I'll get you some water,' said Jason.

'Just before you do, tell me, has Jean ever hurt you? Has he done things to you, Jason?'

Jason shook his head.

'You probably don't want to talk about it, do you. Maybe get that water for me, and then we can talk.'

Jason paused, then walked up the stairs to the kitchen. He found a cup on the draining board. He filled it with water from the tap. He opened the kitchen cabinet. He took out a candle.

In the cellar, Anita looked anxiously around the room. Her eyes darted from a dusty shelf to an old bookcase.

'There it is!' she said.

She moved quickly and slipped the screwdriver into her hand, then she sat on the chair.

She could see Jason's feet coming down the stairs. He held the water and the candle.

'Jason, thank you.'

He stood next to her, holding the candle and the water.

'I didn't want to come here,' she said. 'This really isn't your fault. Cain told me how much you love the theatre. What's your favourite play?'

Jason looked up at the ceiling. He looked like someone thinking about a question.

Suddenly, Anita stood up and thrust the screwdriver into his eye. Jason let out a terrible scream. His hands went quickly to his face. Anita withdrew the object and then thrust it into the other eye. He fell to his knees, howling.

Anita dropped the bloody object and then walked quickly up the stairs. She searched through the kitchen drawers. She grabbed a large kitchen knife. She walked down into the cellar. Methodically. Jason was curled into a ball on the floor.

'Jason, I'm going to kill you. I'm going to kill you and cut your stupid head off!'

She stabbed hard into his back. He rolled over and flung his arms wildly to protect himself. She moved away quickly and then struck deep into his abdomen and chest. Jason's body bled profusely. The floor was wet with his blood. His life flowed out unstopped.

Anita was utterly drained. There was nothing left of her. She dropped the knife. She walked up the stairs again.

She searched for keys. She found them hanging from a nail at the side of the kitchen cupboard. She sleepwalked down the stairs. She neared the door that entombed Ham. The first key she tried was the one. She pulled the heavy door as hard as she could. When it opened, she saw Ham lying on his back on the floor. His eyes were open and staring, his expression frozen in despair.

'Ham!' she cried. She collapsed and held him.

'Ham! Wake up! What's wrong with you?'

She could hold back no longer. Her body was wracked with a flood of desperate tears.

22

Donna lay on her mattress. Carlos stood at the window. He could see the sun shining on the hills. He could see the white clouds drifting in the blue sky. He turned and looked at Donna. She was almost spent. Her body was flat and thin. She was dying. Someone needed to save them. Someone needed to save them from this torment.

'Jan's not going to release us,' he said quietly to Donna.

Donna turned her head towards the wall.

'Carlos, the other day I wrote about you, Jean and Madelaine. And me. I wrote about us doing something. I wrote about us abducting and torturing someone. There was blood. It was awful. I don't know why I did it. It just happened that way.'

She turned her head and faced him. There were tears in her eyes.

'Carlos,' she said, 'come here.' He walked to the bed and lay down next to her. Donna put her arms around him.

'I think I have to keep writing about the torture of this man. Jan is forcing me. Jan is forcing me to do it.' She turned and lay on her back, staring at the ceiling. 'It sounds insane, and I don't understand, but I need to do this. It's going to help us. It's going to help save us.'

Carlos was looking at Donna intensely. 'I hate Jan so much. He's destroying you. I could kill him for what he did to us. What he showed us.'

Donna turned towards him. 'He let Pearl be abused.'

'He's making it up in our minds,' said Carlos. 'None of it is real.'

Donna had tears in her eyes now. 'Pearl is real, Carlos. You know she is. We saw her. She's our daughter, Carlos. We need to listen to Jan. What did he say? We can save her.'

Carlos was silent.

'I'm going further into the other world. We're going there for Jean and Madelaine. We're going there for Pearl. I have to finish the war against the cabal. I have to hurt them. I have to destroy them. That's how we're going to be free.'

23

Cain and Rebecca stood transfixed in their lounge room, looking out the window at the motionless figure of Jean Jambon. Rebecca held Cain's arm tight.

'Do something,' she said.

'Get a knife from the kitchen.'

Rebecca let go of his arm and walked quickly into the kitchen. She opened the drawer. She pulled out a large knife and walked back to Cain. Jean was gone.

'Where is he?' she asked.

'He just disappeared,' said Cain. 'I'm going outside.'

'Stay here!'

'I need to talk to him.'

'You need to stay with me. Stay with me, Cain!'

'If anything happens to me, you need to take the car and get out of here.'

They heard a sudden crash at the front door.

'He's here!' said Cain. 'Go out the back way. Wait for me in the car.'

Jean Jambon walked into the room. He smiled at Cain.

Cain stood motionless next to Rebecca.

'What do you think you are doing?' she said. 'You're breaking into our house. This is our home!'

Jean Jambon looked at Rebecca. He sat down in a chair.

'I don't have any complaint with you, Rebecca. Why don't you take Cain's advice and go and sit in the car?'

Rebecca shook her head. Jean made himself comfortable.

'I have some business with Cain. This man here was warned by me twenty years ago. A very clear and stern warning was given. He ignored it. He ignored it, and now he has to pay a price. Isn't that right, Cain?'

As he finished speaking, he stood up.

Cain moved closer to Rebecca.

Rebecca held out the knife towards Jean.

Jean smiled.

'Put the knife down, Rebecca.'

She held the knife firmly in front of Jean. He came closer.

Rebecca lunged at Jean with the knife. Jean grabbed her hand. He bent it backwards. Rebecca screamed with pain. The knife dropped. As it dropped, Jean caught it with his other hand. He caught it and then thrust it upwards into Cain's abdomen. Jean Jambon sliced the knife sideways. Cain grabbed for his belly and fell to his knees.

Jean Jambon dropped the knife and walked contemptuously into the night.

24

Ham was dead. Anita sat next to him and stroked his hair. He was like a little bird that had fallen from its nest. Poor Ham was just a little bird that had fallen and died.

'My poor Ham,' said Anita. 'My poor Ham. Look what has happened to my poor baby. I should have looked after you better. I should've never got you involved.'

Anita sat with him for a long time. In the darkness. Then she scanned the floor. She searched on her hands and knees. She searched the dusty, bloody floor and found her phone. She keyed the number for the police and stared at it.

'When they come, they're going to ask me questions about Jason. They're going to arrest me. Take me to the station. Lock me up. Send me to the court. All the while, Jean Jambon is out there. He's free while I'm locked up. I can't do that to you, Ham. I need to get you out of here. I need to take you home. I'm going to take you home, Ham. I'm going to take you home, but I need to go there first. I'll be back, Ham. I won't leave you here.'

Anita looked around one more time. At the misery and carnage. She walked up the stairs into the kitchen. She walked to the back of the house looking for the bathroom. She found it and walked inside. She looked in the mirror. She stared at the face. 'I'm someone else now,' she said to her reflection. She looked down at the basin. She ran hot water, picked up the soap and washed her bloody hands. She scrubbed the blood away from her fingers. Splashed water on her face. She dried it with the sleeve of her shirt. She walked back out into the kitchen and pushed the cellar door closed. She walked down the hallway. She opened the front door and then closed it behind her. The night was empty and cold. A chill wind blew. She needed to get home fast.

25

Rebecca looked down at the body of Cain. The body of Cain had emptied out its life. He was just an empty thing now.

The murderous form of Jean Jambon had exploded into her life and left behind the corpse of her husband.

There wasn't much to do now. She was an empty doll. She was a doll who was tethered only slightly to this earth.

She walked outside. Through the broken door. The storm was still howling. The storm was empty too. Just material forces. No emotion. Absence. She tried her phone. No reception. Reception was bad up here. It didn't matter. She was truly alone.

She walked into the bedroom. Stripped back the bedclothes. She pulled off the top sheet. Walked into the kitchen. She covered Cain with the sheet. She gazed at his shrouded body. She wept. She wept for a long time. She wept for Cain and for herself. Then the tears ended as suddenly as they began.

She lifted the shroud and looked through his pockets searching for the keys. She found them and walked to the car. There was nothing to take with her. She was leaving it all behind.

She started the engine. She switched on the lights. The drive through the forest was long and lonely. She reached the main road. She headed for the nearest town. It wasn't too far away.

It was late when she arrived. The police station was closed. She tried her phone again. This time, there was reception. 'My husband has been murdered,' she said. She gave the address. Someone would be there. Could she wait in the car? She tilted the seat back. She was so spent.

When the police arrived, they took some details. They asked if they could help her in any way. She said no. Said she wanted to be left alone. She didn't need police help.

They would go to the house in the mountains. They would go there and see the body of Cain. They would call an ambulance, or something like that. It didn't matter. They would need to investigate the scene. Take some photos. That kind of thing. It didn't matter. They couldn't do anything she needed. She needed to be home. They said they would speak to her tomorrow. In her house. Or she could go to the police station. What was the point?

After the police had spoken to her, she was left standing near her car. It was very early morning. Too early for light yet. That ugly, sickening time when nothing has been formed yet. That time when things are ill-shaped and unclear. She looked around. There were derelict houses. Rubbish on the street. Rolling down the street as rubbish always does. A burnt-out car in the distance. She walked for a little. Just to clear her head. She walked but soon grew tired. There was nothing new here. It was the same everywhere. Exhaustion. Decay. The fall. She stopped and looked back at her car.

'I need to get home,' she said to herself. 'Before the sun rises. I need to get home and go to bed. I need to go to bed for a very long time.'

When she arrived home, she was ready to collapse. She walked through the house as if she wasn't even there. Rebecca was becoming a ghost. Fading away into her surroundings. The walls. The furniture. The paintings. She might remain in her paintings. That probably wasn't enough. That probably wasn't going to get her through what was coming.

She walked to the bedroom. She opened the drawer of her bedside table. Inside were some pills in a plastic bag.

She walked into the kitchen. Pulled out the vodka. She got a glass from the cupboard. She sat on the couch. She looked out the window. The sun was rising. Over the blackened trees and the ruins.

'They will find my body,' she said to herself. 'My body will be a lump on the couch. I'll be gone. I'm almost there.'

26

Donna was talking to Carlos. She said she was full of regret. She regretted the way that she had tried to free herself with hateful poison. The abduction and the torture. The feeling that it should be filmed. The desire to hurt another and be vengeful. She said it led nowhere. The cell had not gone away. She was still a prisoner with Carlos. She was still imprisoned and separated from Madelaine and Jean.

'I'm not going to free Jean and Madelaine with this story,' she said.

That's when Donna started crying.

'I'm not the same,' said Donna. 'I am not the same person that I was before now.'

Donna got up and found the words that she had written. She found the words about the abduction and the plans for the abduction. She found the discussion about the abduction and then the beatings. And then the bloodletting.

'I thought these words were the door to another realm. I thought they would open, and Jean and Madelaine would step out through them. I thought I had made a magic opening in the veil between this world and the other. But these words aren't a door.'

Donna ripped up the pages and the words. She closed the opening that was never an opening.

'I'm not going to escape through words. I'm not going to escape through a door made from words.'

She looked at the sleeping Carlos.

'Carlos,' she said. 'Carlos, Madelaine and Jean. I'm going to find the real door.'

Donna walked to the window. The tiny window in her cell.

'Jan has the key,' she said. 'Jan is the key to the door.'

27

Anita could hardly walk. She was so traumatised. The car was parked near the theatre. There was no one around. No one to see her cold, shaking body. Or her mind outside of her body. Floating.

She got in the car and turned on the heater. She started the engine. Turned her car lights on.

Ham was dead in the old hoarder's house. The old hoarder was dead, too. 'I'm a killer now,' she said.

Anita drove her car home. It was a long way. When she arrived, the lights in the house were on.

She paused in the car. She looked around. A stray dog walked by. She watched it walk by.

She walked to her front door. The door was wrong. She pushed it aside. She was ready for anything now.

She walked into the living area. Sitting in a chair facing her was Jean Jambon.

'Have a seat, Anita,' he said.

'You don't offer me a seat in my own house,' she replied. 'You're not welcome here, Jean. There's the door. It's open. You need to stand up and walk through it.'

'That's not very friendly, Anita. Maybe you need to sit down and rest. Why don't you sit down right here, and we can resume our chat. We were talking about a friend of yours. I think his name was Cain.'

'I'm calling the police.'

'You know I went to see Cain. His wife was there too. She tried to stab me.'

'You have that effect on people.'

Anita had her phone in her hand. She dialled the number.

'That's not going to help you,' said Jean.

Anita walked away from him. She moved into the kitchen. She pulled out a drawer and found a knife.

'I have an intruder in my house,' Anita said to the person on the phone.

'Cain's wife had a knife like that,' said Jean. 'She tried to stab me, but she slipped.'

'He's here in front of me'

'She slipped badly, and she stabbed Cain. Fatally, I think.'

Anita nodded in reply to something someone said on the phone. Anita held out the knife in the direction of Jean. She moved slowly out of the kitchen and into the hallway.

'I wanted to talk to you about our son. But you don't seem in a talkative mood. That's a shame because there's something I need to tell you, Anita. Our son is a bad man. You see, I knew this would happen. I knew he would turn out to be a very bad man. And you brought him into this world, Anita. So I blame you. I'm very unhappy about that. I'm very unhappy that you have done something so terrible as to give birth to a monster.

Don't you think you should answer for that, Anita? I mean, don't you think there needs to be some kind of retribution? You can't just give birth to a monster and then expect to go free, can you?'

While he talked, Anita edged her way down the hallway. At the end of the hallway was the bathroom. She slipped inside and quickly locked the door. She listened intently.

Jean Jambon had stopped. It was quiet.

Anita sat on the edge of the bath. She gripped the knife. Her senses were focused. She listened with all her being. Moments passed. Her grip on the knife began to loosen. She stood up. She unlocked the door. She opened it slightly and looked down the hallway. Standing in the kitchen, looking directly at her was the figure of a cop.

Jean was gone. She pushed open the door. Anita walked towards the cop. She dropped the knife and began to cry.

28

Jan dragged Donna and Carlos out of their cells. Jan had to explain to them that they were nothing. That they didn't really exist. Not in any way that was important.

Donna turned her head away from Jan.

'You're not listening to me, Donna. I thought you were special. I thought I could reveal my secrets to you. But you can't listen. Human ears are full of garbage.'

'I don't know what you want!' yelled Donna.

Donna was kicking and fighting as she was tied down to the table. Carlos was lying there passively.

Jan took them forward again. Jan got inside their heads with pain. Jan showed them Pearl again.

Donna and Carlos are in a house. It's their house. Donna and Carlos are inside their house, and they are playing with Pearl. They are playing with blocks. Pearl and Donna are building a little castle. They are building a little castle that has little men on the battlements. And inside the little castle, there is a scene. They are making a little scene with the figurines. They are making a little medieval scene reminiscent of the manger.

Jan pauses the scene. He moves the focus closer to Pearl. The screen in Donna's mind fills with the image of Pearl. Her eyes. The sweet eyes of Pearl, sending love to Donna.

Jan turns the screws a little tighter now. He tells Donna and Carlos something. He tells them Pearl is coming tomorrow. Pearl will be at the farm tomorrow. They should get themselves ready.

Donna and Carlos don't know where they are for a moment. They don't know if they are in a dreamscape with Pearl or if they are in a hell scape with Jan.

'Wake them up,' said Jan. 'Take them away.'

When they got back to their cell, they both collapsed onto the mattress.

'What are we going to do?' whispered Carlos.

'He said Pearl was coming tomorrow,' whispered Donna.

'Pearl isn't real. Pearl is something Jan made up.'

'We can see her tomorrow.'

'Pearl isn't a living being, Donna.'

'I can feel her, Carlos. I know she's real.'

'Donna, think about it. You have never given birth. Have you?'

'I don't know. I don't know for sure.'

Carlos held Donna tight. He repeated her name softly.

'I love Pearl. I want to see her. We're going to see her, Carlos.'

Carlos kissed her forehead and stroked her hair. He reached down and pulled the blanket over them.

Tomorrow, they would see her. That's what Donna said as she drifted off to sleep.

29

Pearl appeared in the early morning. She stood between two beings of light. There was one on each side of her. Pearl stood there, looking at Carlos and Donna. She stood there next to the beings and the barn. Jan stood next to Donna and Carlos. He restrained them with his power. They all stood outside in the morning on the farm. It was a farm morning like any other, except that this was a strange farm morning. This was a farm morning with grass and cows and barns and farmhouses. And aliens and children who didn't exist. Little Pearl was here. It was impossible.

'That's not really her,' said Carlos.

'Pearl,' said Donna. 'Mummy's here.'

'Please, Donna.'

'Mummy can see you.'

Pearl raised her hand in a greeting to Donna and Carlos. Donna lifted her hand and waved too.

'Let me go to her,' said Donna.

'You're not ready,' said Jan. 'You're not a mother yet.'

'But she's here,' said Donna. 'What do you mean I'm not a mother? I can see her. That's my child.'

Carlos turned and looked at Donna. He took her hand and held it.

'I brought Pearl from the future,' said Jan. 'But she isn't here. She shimmers like that because she's not here.'

The beings of light moved forward, and Pearl moved forward with them.

'Pearl has something important to say to you,' said Jan. 'Try to listen without anything in your mind.'

'I'm waiting over there,' said Pearl.

With that, she turned and walked towards the barn. She walked towards the barn with the beings of light.

Jan smiled. He told Donna to remember what Pearl had said.

'I don't understand what she means,' said Donna.

'Don't listen to him,' said Carlos.

'Look over there,' said Jan. He pointed to the barn. The beings took Pearl inside the barn. They walked through the barn door. They closed the barn door behind them.

Donna could hear something. Donna could hear the voice of Pearl.

'Mummy!' That's what Pearl called out.

Donna begged Jan to let her go.

'She's calling me. She needs me!'

Jan said he would let her go if Donna promised to do something.

'Anything!' She yelled

'You need to resume the terror,' said Jan.

'I can't!'

'You need to resume the terror so that you can save Pearl. You've seen what will happen to her.'

'Don't do this to me! Why are you doing this to me?'

Jan moved closer to her. Very close. And spoke into her whole being.

'Save her,' he said.

At that moment, Carlos broke free from Jan's power. He ran to the barn. He got to the barn door. He opened the barn door.

'Carlos, stop!' yelled Donna.

'He's gone,' said Jan.

'Let me go! I want Pearl! Let me go! I want to see Carlos!'

'He's gone,' said Jan. 'Don't you remember that door? You know that door. He's gone through the same door as Madelaine and Jean. Why don't you go and see?'

Jan freed Donna from her bondage. Donna walked unsteadily towards the barn. She opened the door. Inside was light. Just light. That's all she could see.

'Pearl?' she called out.

She looked around. She saw Jan standing at the barn door.

'Pearl is here, Donna. Pearl is waiting for you. But you're not ready yet. You need to come with me and show me your terror.'

The hospital assistants walked past Jan and into the light. They took Donna's hand. They guided her out. Donna let herself be guided.

She was led back to the surgery. She was laid on the table. Jan placed his hand on her forehead.

'This will hurt you,' he said.

Jan took Donna way back to the dark days. Donna was always being taken back by Jan.

Jan says humans are disgusting. It's alright to exploit and abuse them. Like when Jan creeps around little Donna's bedroom at night. Lifting her up and transporting her through walls. She's done all that before. Jan does it again.

Jan again takes little Donna out through the walls of her bedroom. Jan takes Donna into an alien craft. Jan takes her down to the hive. Jan takes Donna down into the hive where the other little children are. Jan tells Donna that Pearl will come to her when she does the right thing. Jan tells Donna what the right thing is. Jan does that by showing her some people. The people are in a chamber. Inside the chamber, Donna can see the walls of a house. It's the house of the abduction. Carlos, Madelaine and Jean are there too. They are in the farmhouse, waiting for Donna to arrive.

Jan cups Donna in his gigantic hand. He gently places her in the scene. Jan tells Donna that she knows what to do. Jan tells Donna that she needs to finish the task. She needs to finish the terror task.

She's big Donna now. Big Donna tells Jean and the others to follow her. They go into the room. The room with the abducted man. Jean has got his phone out. Madelaine is holding the knife. Carlos is holding the man. They are all looking at Donna. They look at Donna, and she knows what to say. She talks to the sad abductee who has committed crimes against the earth. She lays it on the line.

'We've tried everything, but it's not possible to go forward without violence. We are acting on behalf of the earth. We love this earth. We love this earth, and we love you, too. Yes, that's right, we love you, but we condemn you. We condemn you for all the criminal actions you have committed against this planet.'

'This is a statement,' said Jean. 'This is a statement of love. Not of hate. We are committing this act out of love for the earth.'

'There has to be some sacrifice,' said Donna. 'There has to be sacrifice so that the destruction can stop. This is sacrificial violence. This is giving up someone for the sake of others. I want you to understand what this means. What we have to give in order for the planet to be saved. I'm going to show you what you have to give for this earth.'

Donna took a bottle from her pocket. The room filled with the smell of petrol.

The man struggled against Jean. He looked terrified.

'Carlos,' said Donna, 'film me!'

Donna emptied the contents of the container over her body. She reached inside her pocket. She pulled out a lighter. She lit the fuel. Her whole body caught fire.

30

Anita was an exhausted woman in tears in front of a cop. There was no hiding her pain.

'I came home and he was here. I can't cope with this.'

There were two cops in the room. One was looking through Anita's kitchen. The other stood next to her.

'We need to ask you some questions,' he said, 'Take your time.'

'His name is Jean Jambon,' she said. 'You need to find him. He's murdered someone I know. He might have killed Rebecca. You need to find Rebecca.'

'Where can we find Rebecca?'

'I don't know where she is. Go to her home. I know her address.'

'What is her address?'

'I want you to take me there. I want to see her. I know something has happened to her.'

'It might be better if you stay here.'

'I don't want to stay here. I'm on my own. I've been traumatised. Can't you see that? I need to see my friend!'

'Tell us what happened here first.'

'I told you. It's Jean Jambon. He's dangerous. You need to find him. I'm not safe. He was here. He trespassed into my house. He threatened me.'

'How did he threaten you?'

'He said he was going to punish me. I can't explain it. He said I should be punished for something I did.'

'What was that?'

'You won't understand. He hates me. He wants to kill me!'

The cop took a breath.

'Do you need to take anything with you?'

'To where?'

'We're going to take you to your friend's house. There will be a team here later to investigate.'

'I'm going like this.'

Anita stood up. As she did so, she turned and looked at the cop in the kitchen. He looked at Anita. She became expressionless. Her mind started floating away from her body.

The cop was Jean Jambon.

'Officer,' she said to the other cop, 'I just remembered that there was something in the bathroom I didn't show you.'

She led him down the hallway to the bathroom. The cop entered. Anita moved close to him.

'I need to talk to you about that other officer,' she whispered.

'What about him?'

'He's not really a cop.'

'He's a police officer.'

'I know him,' she whispered intently.

'What do you know?'

'He's Jean Jambon.'

'No, he's not'

'What's his name then?'

The cop paused to think. His face was blank. He looked a little concerned.

'I can't recall.'

'What?'

'He's new. He told me his name. But I can't recall it.'

'What's going on here?' Anita's voice was rising.

'Is everything alright down there?'

Anita froze when she heard the voice of Jean Jambon.

'Answer him,' she whispered.

'Just a minute,' replied the cop. 'Everything's fine.'

'Have you seen him before?' asked Anita.

'No.'

'And you don't know his name. What's wrong with you?'

'Come with me,' said the cop. 'We need to sort this out.'

'I'm not going out there.'

'We're going to sort this out. Nothing is going to happen.'

They walked down the hallway. The cop was in front. They entered the living area of the house. Jean was standing there. He had his gun out.

'You've been talking too much, Anita,' he said. 'Let's go and pay your friend a visit. You can talk some more there.'

Jean Jambon turned to the cop. He shot him twice. The cop fell like a sack.

Jean walked over to Anita and took her by the arm.

'We're going,' he said.

31

Donna lay on the table in Jan's so-called hospital, recovering from her own suicide.

'This isn't a gospel story,' said Jan. 'You're not saving anyone with sacrificial acts.'

Donna was helped slowly to her feet. She walked badly. Donna was unsteady. She turned towards Jan.

'Where's Carlos?' she said. 'He needs to be here.'

'Don't you remember? There was a barn, Donna. There was a barn, and Pearl went inside the barn. What did Carlos do then?'

'No, that didn't really happen.'

Jan just looked at her and said nothing.

'No, that was something you made me believe.'

'Carlos is gone,' said Jan. He went into the barn. He went into the barn with Pearl, and he didn't come back.'

'Stop doing this to me!'

'The barn is there, Donna.'

Jan pointed in the direction of the old barn. It was there. She could see it.

'I'm not looking at it. That's just an old barn. I don't like it. Why are you doing this?'

Jan reached over and touched Donna's hand.

'Come with me.'

Donna and Jan walked to the old barn.

'Open the door, Donna,' Jan said.

Donna opened the door. The light was still there. The light was all she could see. Jan led Donna into the light.

'You want to see Carlos, don't you?'

Jan pointed up to the ceiling. Which didn't really exist. Nothing existed inside the barn except the light.

Donna was really on the edge now. There was nothing here that made any sense.

'I don't want to see him now,' she said.

'Yes, you do,' said Jan.

With that, Carlos appeared by her side. He was holding Pearl's hand. They were shimmering.

'I can't talk to you, Donna,' he said. 'I'm not here.'

'You're not here,' said Donna. 'That's what Jan said.'

'I found her. She's here. She's with me.'

'I know, Carlos. I can see you. What happened to you?'

'I'm here. I don't know.'

Donna turned to Jan.

'Where is he? Where are they?'

'Carlos and Pearl have gone, Donna. Carlos and Pearl went through the door. You know they did. I want to show you something else.'

Jan pointed upwards. In the light was Jean Le Reel and Madelaine. They were floating in the light.

'No!' gasped Donna.

'Your friends,' said Jan.

There were tears in Donna's eyes. It had been so long since she had seen them. They were glowing. They were beings of light. They looked calm and peaceful.

'Jean! Madelaine!' called Donna.

Jan touched her hand again.

'They wanted to come here and say hello to you,' said Jan. 'They wanted to see their Donna before you go.'

'I don't want to go.' Donna said.

Her loved ones were shimmering and starting to fade. They were fading in the light. Soon, nothing was left of them at all.

Donna stood alone in the barn.

Once there was emotion and light. Now there was just a barn. A dusty old wooden barn. There was nobody at all. Not even Jan.

She looked around.

She walked through the barn door. Outside was daytime. It was light. Just normal human light. The light of the earth.

Donna looked around. The trees. The grass. The fences. The buildings. All empty of strange meaning. Just material things.

Donna walked into the house. Nothing she had seen before was there. It was just an old farmhouse now. No operating theatre. No beds to lie on. No beds to be bound to.

She walked through the house. The room that was her cell was just an old room full of junk. The whole house had been abandoned years ago.

Donna had been abandoned. She was abandoned. Donna was a cracked thing who needed to recover.

Donna walked out of the house. She walked down the old driveway. Donna walked out of the farm gate. She walked down the road.

She headed for the mountain.

32

Jean and Anita drove in the cop car. Jean had the car locked, so Anita couldn't jump out. Anita could see what was happening. Jean was a killer and out of control.

'We're not going to see Rebecca,' said Jean. 'I've changed my mind. We're going on a little country drive. We're going to the place where our Jean was last seen.'

'Seen by who?'

'You don't need to worry about that.'

'What are you going to do to him?'

'Let's be honest. You know what I'm going to do.'

'Why do you want to do this?'

'You don't need to know, Anita. But I do want you to see it when it happens.'

Anita turned her head and looked at him.

'Something will stop you.'

Jean smiled.

They drove on through the suburbs that slowly ebbed away into the countryside.

'When we get there, Anita, we'll look for the boy,' said Jean. 'He'll be around somewhere.'

Anita said nothing.

'I know you desperately want to see him. I know you want to save him. So you'll help me. We will find him. The rest will take care of itself.'

She remained silent. Her heart was pounding. She looked out the window and watched the countryside go by.

They arrived at the foot of a mountain. Jean got out of the car. He held the gun. He opened Anita's door and waved the gun in the direction of the house.

Jean pushed open the front door. The house was empty.

They walked into the living room. There were cups on the table. There were drawings and some writing.

'Sit down, Anita.' Jean waved the gun in the direction of the sofa.

Jean picked up the writing and read it. He looked at the drawings. He lifted the cup to his nose and took in the scent.

'Looks like our boy went for a little nature walk. Did you know our boy was a nature lover? I didn't. It's good to discover things about your children. It's good to see them out and about discovering the world.'

Anita had to lie down. She stretched out on the sofa. She closed her eyes.

Jean was walking around the room. Taking it all in.

'I hope you're feeling fit,' he said. We have a long climb ahead of us.'

Anita had fallen asleep.

Jean sat down on a chair facing her.

'When you wake up, Anita, we will be going for a walk. Probably the last walk of your life. Get some rest. Enjoy your dreams.'

33

It was lonely now for Donna to be on this road. Donna was trying to put things back together inside her head, but her head was split apart. Her head was split into little bits that wanted to go this way and that.

She walked by little creeks rushing down through reeds and willows. She walked by green fields and pines that whispered in the wind. They weren't saying anything. There were no words here.

Donna trod on and on. She went on in the heat at the closing of the day and the closing of the night. She found shelter in the ground, the branches and the leaves.

Her journey on the road weakened her so much.

There was nothing else to live for, that's what she said. There was nothing else to live for.

She kept walking to the mountain. Through the flat lands. The undulating fields. The steep, tree-lined ridges. The awkward rocky climb.

Then she came to the place where her friends were taken by the door. Where she and Carlos were taken by Jan. And at the top of the mountain, where the moon had touched the earth, she could see in the distance an immense glow of light.

It was the light of Jan. He stood in a doorway. He stood in the doorway of the barn.

Jan stood on the mountain top and looked at Donna. He looked at her free body.

He lifted up his hand and pointed his palm upwards. He slowly moved it from left to right.

'Take in the scene, Donna,' he said.

Donna took in the death scene. Donna took in the corpses of Anita and Jean Jambon. Lying face down in the earth. Blood pooled around their bodies. A gun on the ground nearby.

'They died like that, Donna,' he said. 'They died in confusion and desperation. I tried to tell them not to come too close. But they knew. They knew I had Jean. Your Jean.'

Donna looked at the barn in disbelief.

'I want to see him,' said Donna.

'He's waiting for you, Donna,' said Jan.

'Why don't you bring him out?'

'You need to come inside.'

With that, Donna walked slowly towards the barn and past the two corpses on the ground.

She walked through the barn doors and into the pure and awful light.

Jan was just a voice now. Jan guided Donna with his voice.

Donna moved through the light. She reached out and found a little hand. She found Pearl's hand. She found the feeling hand of Pearl, who guided Donna down into the hive.

Inside the hive walls were countless human bodies. She had seen human bodies before, but not ones stored for future use.

She slowed down. It was too awful to go on. Nobody should have to go on towards what was there.

She stood motionless and stared at the bodies of Carlos, Madelaine and Jean. Tears streamed down her face. She seemed impaled by grief. She stood there forever in that cold corpse box.

Pearl was by her side, still. She raised her hand and placed it on Donna. Donna turned and looked down. She took Pearl's hand.

The light slowly lifted to reveal Jan standing next to a table. It was the old table. The old, hateful table from the bad times.

Jan held the needle in his hand. The old penetrating needle that stuck Donna in her mind so hard.

Donna walked towards Jan. She still held the hand of Pearl. Donna lifted her onto the table.

Jan smiled.

Donna turned quickly and grasped the hand that held the nccdlc. Shc graspcd his slimy hand and pushcd thc nccdlc back into his throat.

Jan gasped and fell to the ground. Black ooze spurted from his neck.

Donna picked up Pearl and retraced her steps.

As she walked, the light began to fail. It fell fast on Donna and her Pearl.

The doorway seemed an eternity away. Donna walked on with Pearl towards the light while being dragged down by the weighty darkness.

As the darkness grew, so did her fatigue.

It was so hard to move now, through this morass of deep despair.

34

It was a cold morning when Donna and Pearl awoke. They lay in the clearing at the top of the mountain.

Around them were the bodies of Jean Jambon and Anita.

A slight breeze was blowing. It blew dark ash towards them. It blew dark ash towards them from the huge ash mound in front of them.

The ash pile of the barn.

Donna looked at Pearl, then held her tight.

Donna could feel Pearl's heartbeat. She had one heart.

'We need to go,' said Donna.

Donna and Pearl walked away from the death zone and towards the new Earth.

There was a long way to go.

34

[illegible]

www.ingramcontent.com/pod-product-compliance
Lightning Source LLC
LaVergne TN
LVHW030913080826
845145LV00010B/2872

* 9 7 8 1 7 6 4 4 6 1 3 0 6 *